D1385494

This book belongs to:

....

....

....

Retold by Gaby Goldsack
Illustrated by Ruth Galloway (Advocate)
Designed by Blue Sunflower Creative

Language consultant: Betty Root

ISBN 1-84461-309-7

Marks and Spencer p.l.c.
PO Box 3339
Chester, CH99 9QS
www.marksandspencer.com

MARKS &
SPENCER

The Elves and
the Shoemaker

Helping your Child to Read

Learning to read is an exciting challenge for most children. From a very early age, sharing story books with children, talking about the pictures and guessing what might happen next are all very important parts of the reading experience.

Sharing reading

Set aside a regular quiet time to share reading with younger children, or to be on hand to encourage older children as they develop into independent readers.

First Readers are intended to encourage and support the early stages of learning to read. They present well-loved tales that children will happily listen to again and again. Familiarity helps children to identify some of the words and phrases.

When you feel your child is ready to move on a little, encourage them to join in so that you read the story aloud together. Always pause to talk about the pictures. The easy-to-read speech bubbles in **First Readers** provide an excellent 'joining-in' activity. The bright, clear illustrations and matching text will help children to understand the story.

Building confidence

In time, children will want to read *to* you. When this happens, be patient and give continual praise. They may not read all the words correctly, but children's substitutions are often very good guesses.

The repetition in each book is particularly helpful for building confidence. If your child cannot read a particular word, go back to the beginning of the sentence and read it together so the meaning is not lost. Most importantly, do not continue if your child is tired or simply in need of a change.

Reading aloud

The next step is to ask your child to read aloud to you. This does require patience and perseverance. Remember to give lots of encouragement and praise.

Together with other simple stories, **First Readers** will ensure that children will find reading an enjoyable and rewarding experience.

Once upon a time there was a shoemaker and his wife. The shoemaker worked very hard. But they were very poor.

One day, all the shoemaker had left was one small piece of leather.

"I will only be able to make one pair of shoes," said the shoemaker.

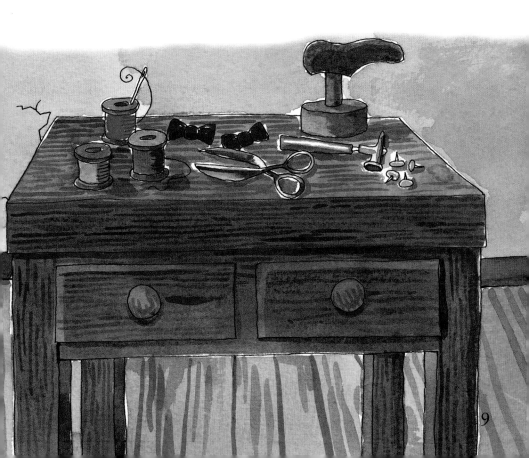

The shoemaker cut out a pair of shoes.
He left them on his workbench to sew
the next morning.

The next morning, the shoemaker was surprised. He found a pair of shoes on his workbench.

They were perfect. But the shoemaker did not know who had sewn them.

That day, a rich lady came into the shop and put on the shoes.

"They are a perfect fit," said the rich lady. She gave the shoemaker a big bag of money.

They are a perfect fit.

Now the shoemaker had money to buy leather for two pairs of shoes.

The shoemaker cut out two pairs of shoes. He left them on his workbench to sew the next morning.

The next morning, the shoemaker was surprised. He found two pairs of shoes on his workbench.

"They are perfect!" said his wife.

That day, a rich man came into the shop. He bought both pairs of shoes.

He gave the shoemaker two big bags of money.

The shoemaker was very happy.

Now he had enough money to buy leather to make four pairs of shoes.

17

Night after night, the same thing happened.

The shoemaker cut out the leather and left it on the workbench. Every morning he found perfect shoes in its place.

But the shoemaker still did not know
who was sewing the shoes.

One night, the shoemaker and his wife
hid in the workshop.

They waited to see who would come.

Sssh!

At midnight, two tiny elves ran in.
Their clothes were very old.

They jumped onto the workbench and
started to sew. They did not stop until
the last shoe was made.

"We must make the elves a present," said the shoemaker to his wife.

So the shoemaker made two pairs of tiny shoes. His wife made two tiny suits.

It took them a very long time.

One night, they left the shoes and suits on the workbench. Then they hid and waited to see what would happen.

At midnight, the two tiny elves ran in.
They jumped up onto the workbench.
They were surprised to see the tiny
clothes and shoes.

We like our clothes.

They put on their new clothes and shoes. They were very happy.

They liked the clothes and shoes.

The shoemaker and his wife never saw the elves again. But they did not mind. The elves had brought them good luck.

From that day on, the shoemaker
worked harder than ever.

And they were never poor again.

Read and Say

How many of these words can you say?
The pictures will help you. Look back in
your book and see if you can find the
words in the story.

wife

shoemaker

money

shoes

workbench

elves

rich lady

clothes

rich man

Titles in this series,
subject to availability:

Beauty and the Beast
Chicken-Licken
Cinderella
The Elves and the Shoemaker
The Emperor's New Clothes
The Enormous Turnip
The Gingerbread Man
Goldilocks and the Three Bears
Hansel and Gretel
Jack and the Beanstalk
Joseph's Coat of Many Colours
Little Red Riding Hood
Noah's Ark and other Bible Stories
Rapunzel
Rumpelstiltskin
Sleeping Beauty
Snow White and the Seven Dwarfs
The Three Billy Goats Gruff
The Three Little Pigs
The Ugly Duckling